The Final Game

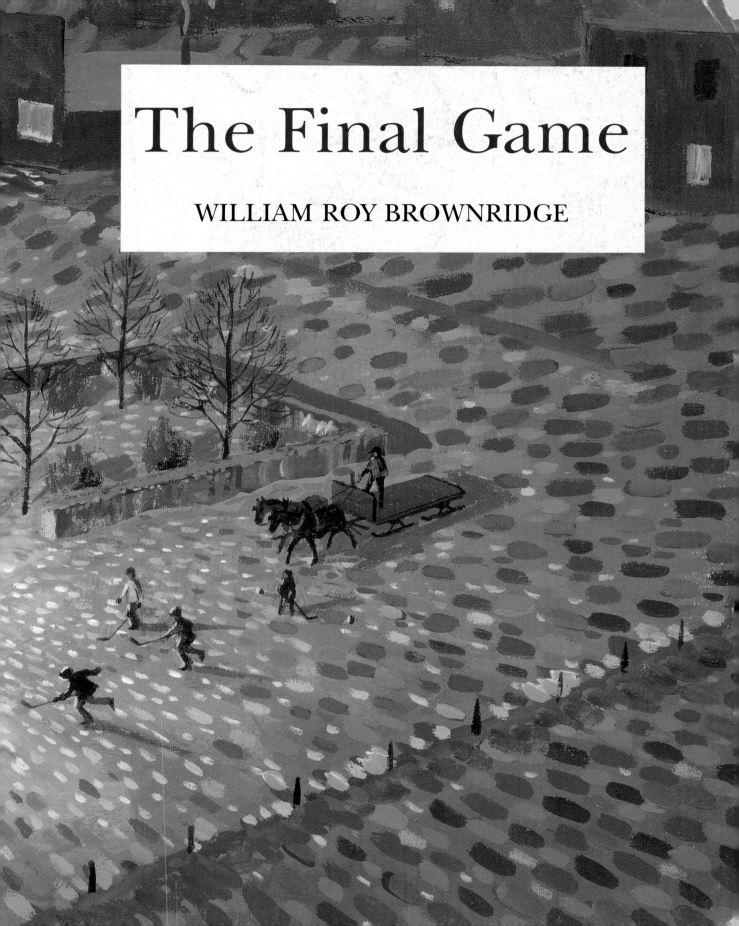

The Final Game

WILLIAM ROY BROWNRIDGE

When I was a boy growing up on the prairies, hockey was the most important thing in my life. I had a crippled leg and foot, so I couldn't wear skates. But that didn't matter. I could play goal in my moccasins, so my teammates called me Moccasin Danny.

Our hockey team was called the Wolves. I joined the team late in the season, along with my friends Petou and Anita. Petou was small but fast. Anita, who could play as well as any boy, was the first girl to join the league.

At first Petou, Anita and I played well and were part of the team. But whenever we lost a game, some of the Wolves began to grumble. Travis, who was our best forward, called us "the wimps" and said we weren't good enough to play on the team. Our coach, Mr. Matteau, told Travis to stop complaining and look after his own game.

So instead of complaining, Travis ignored us. He never passed the puck to Anita or Petou in practice, not even in games.

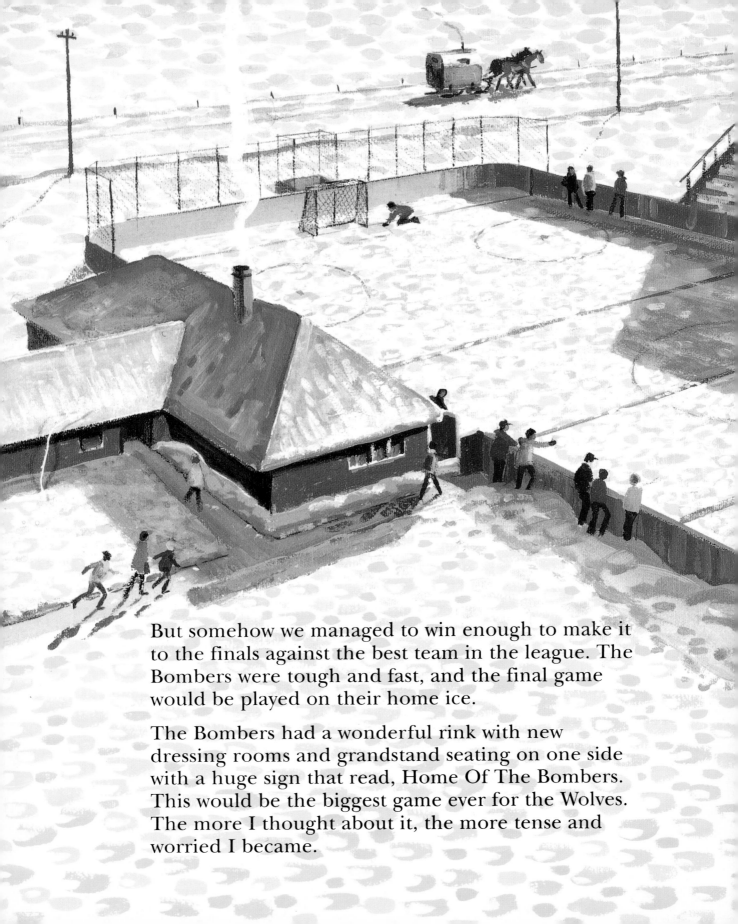

But somehow we managed to win enough to make it to the finals against the best team in the league. The Bombers were tough and fast, and the final game would be played on their home ice.

The Bombers had a wonderful rink with new dressing rooms and grandstand seating on one side with a huge sign that read, Home Of The Bombers. This would be the biggest game ever for the Wolves. The more I thought about it, the more tense and worried I became.

One morning before the final game, the piercing hoot of the train whistle woke me with a start. I jumped out of bed and ran to the window. Over the rooftops a plume of white smoke billowed in the distance. My heart leapt. I had forgotten! My brother was on that train. Bob was a star left-winger for the Toronto Maple Leafs. He was coming home to rest an injured shoulder.

I arrived at the station late and out of breath. Coach Matteau, all the members of the Wolves and half the town were there.

After the cheers and noisy greetings had died down, I heard the coach say, "Bob, the team has their final playoff game tomorrow. Would you come to our practice this afternoon?"

I could barely see my brother through the crowd. "Sure, coach," he said. Then he spotted me. "But first I'm going to visit my family."

The crowd moved aside and he walked towards me, whisked me up in one arm and hugged me tight. He looked like a hero in his jacket with the famous Maple Leaf crest.

That afternoon, as Bob and the coach skated out to practice, a ripple of excitement ran through the team. Everyone was thrilled to have a real pro teach us. At first, Bob worked the team through some passing and shooting drills. All the Wolves played their best. But in our practice game, Travis tried to be the star. Instead of passing to Petou, Travis attempted to stickhandle through the whole team, and was checked and lost the puck. "What a puck hog," Petou muttered.

At the end of the practice, Mr. Matteau called the team together. "You've shown Bob and I that you have the skills to win tomorrow, but the question is: Can you play as a team? Please think about that when you go home tonight."

The next afternoon, a huge crowd cheered as the two teams took to the ice. The cheering became a roar when Bob, wearing his Leaf jacket, walked to the Wolves' bench.

I crouched in goal, torn between eagerness and fear. A jumble of loud voices called out, "Come on, Wolves!", "Come on, Moccasin Danny!" and "Go Bombers, Go!"

From the opening face-off, our captain Marcel took charge and scored on a give-and-go with a sizzling shot to the goalies' stick side. Then Anita scored in a wild scramble in front of the Bombers' net. We were flying high and leading two to zero.

But in the final moments of the period, one of our defensemen tried to carry the puck out of the Wolves' zone instead of passing. He was checked and the Bombers scored on me. I looked at our bench. Bob and Coach Matteau just shook their heads.

The second period was a battle. The Bombers tried to pick on Anita, roughing and tripping her without drawing a penalty. Finally they cross-checked her to the ice. She came to the bench fighting back tears. Travis yelled out, "What's the matter, wimp? Can't you take it?"

Somehow we held the Bombers off. By the end of the second period we were still leading two to one.

In the dying moments of the third period, we thought we had won. But then the Bomber captain beat our defense and moved in on me home-free. Petou, in a desperate move, tripped him from behind, and the referee whistled a penalty shot. It would be just him and me: the Bomber's top scorer against Moccasin Danny. I felt dizzy. My opponent sneered.

He came at me from centre ice with a burst of speed and blur of stickhandling. Then he whipped a high hard shot to my glove side. I got a piece of it, but the puck dropped into the net behind me. A minute later the buzzer sounded the end of the period. The game was tied. We were going into overtime.

I left the ice, my stomach tied in knots.

The dressing room was quiet. Heads down, we tried to gather our strength. Bob stood and broke the silence. "You're playing well. Keep pressing. Coach Matteau and I just want to make one change. Travis, you join Marcel's line with Petou on the wing."

Travis grinned at Marcel. But, as usual, he ignored Petou.

"Before we go," Bob continued, "I'd like to tell you how I injured my shoulder. We were leading the New York Rangers by one goal and the game was almost over. The Rangers came on a rush and one of our defensemen fell down. I had to back-check against their fastest winger. Just as the Ranger took a pass and was about to score, I managed to lift his stick and the goal was saved. We won the game, but I crashed into the boards at top speed. I had to do whatever I could to help the Leafs. That's what you do when you play this game. You play for the team."

Bob moved behind Travis, patted his back and whispered something in his ear. Then he looked up and said, "Now let's go get 'em!"

The Bombers came at us in waves. I fought off so many shots I started to wonder if there were two pucks instead of one.

One vicious shot glanced off my stick and rolled towards the goal line. Out of nowhere, Anita threw herself flat on the ice and hooked the puck to the corner. What a save!

We quickly counter-attacked with Marcel scooping up the puck and charging to centre ice. He passed to Travis, who broke across the blue line in full flight. Travis stickhandled furiously, but two Bombers pushed him into a corner.

Travis was trapped. Wildly he looked around for another teammate, but no one was in the clear. Just as the Bombers moved in to take the puck, Travis looked over to the goal.

Little Petou, unnoticed, was alone at the open side of the Bombers' net. Quickly Travis whipped a pass across the ice.

Petou coolly tipped it in.

The game was over! We won!

The crowd cheered as Officer Adams presented the North Line cup to our captain Marcel. As the commotion began to die down, I called out, "Hey Travis, what did Bob whisper to you just before we went on the ice?"

The crowd fell silent as all eyes turned to Travis.

Travis shrugged and smiled. "He said, 'Watch for Petou. The Bombers don't cover him.'"

Everyone cheered and laughed. Coach Matteau hoisted Petou on his shoulders and carried him off the ice.

We celebrated long into the night at Chong's Cafe. We didn't want the evening to end. Everyone told and retold their story of the game.

As we finally tumbled out of the cafe, Bob put his arm around Petou and led him over to Travis. "So I guess there are no wimps on this team, are there?" he said.

Travis looked at Petou and nodded. "No wimps — just winners," he answered with a grin.

To my children, David, Leanne, Nancy, Beth and Boyd, for their constant and loving support and a special thanks to David, for his editorial advice.

W.R.B

Copyright © 1997 William Roy Brownridge

Orca Book Publishers gratefully acknowledges the support for our publishing programs provided by the following agencies: the Department of Canadian Heritage, the Canada Council for the Arts, and the British Columbia Ministry Arts Council.
All rights reserved.

First paperback printing, 1998

Orca Book Publishers
PO Box 5626, Station B
Victoria, BC V8R 6S4
Canada

Orca Book Publishers
PO Box 468
Custer, WA 98240-0468
USA

Canadian Cataloguing in Publication Data
Brownridge, William Roy, 1932 –
The final game

ISBN 1-55143-102-5
1. Hockey—Juvenile fiction. I. Title.
PS8553.R694F56 1997   jC813'.54   C97–910429–7
PZ7.B8242Fi 1997

Library of Congress Catalog Card Number: 97-67367

Design by Christine Toller
Printed and bound in Hong Kong

00 99 98   5 4 3 2 1